McCordsville Elementary
Media Center

THE
MILKMAN'S BOY

DONALD HALL

ILLUSTRATIONS BY
GREG SHED

WALKER AND COMPANY
NEW YORK

For Mike Pride
—D. H.

To Mary for all her support
—G. S.

First published in the United States of America in 1997 by Walker Publishing Company, Inc.

Published simultaneously in Canada by Thomas Allen & Son Canada, Limited, Markham, Ontario

Library of Congress Cataloging-in-Publication Data

Hall, Donald, 1928–

The milkman's boy / Donald Hall; illustrations by Greg Shed.

p. cm.

Summary: Tells the story of the Graves Family Dairy, whose three horses pulled the wagons
delivering milk to families in the years before trucks and shopping centers replaced them.

ISBN 0-8027-8463-1 (hardcover). —ISBN 0-8027-8465-8 (reinforced).

[1. Dairying—history—fiction. 2. Milk—Fiction.] I. Shed, Greg, ill. II. Title.

PZ7.H14115Mi 1997 [E]—dc21 97–14170

CIP AC

The illustrations were painted with gouache on canvas. Display type is Dante Titling; text type is Dante Regular.

Book design by Claire B. Counihan

Printed in Hong Kong

10 9

THE HORSES were the best part, for the milkman's boy.
Behind their house in the village of Busterville, next to
the Graves Family Dairy, were stables for the three horses
that pulled the milk wagons: Dolly, Polly, and Fred.

When the horses returned from delivering milk, Paul Graves, who was eleven, fed them each an apple. After the apples were used up in winter, he gave them lumps of sugar.

Polly was his favorite—big, brown, and affectionate. She whinnied when she caught sight of Paul and nuzzled her head against his side—which tickled. Sometimes Polly got two apples. Paul daydreamed about when he would be big enough to deliver milk and spend every morning with Polly.

The whole Graves family worked together to bottle and deliver milk, which they bought in big cans from neighborhood farmers. Paul's father, Henry, delivered one route of milk bottles to people's doorsteps early every morning. Paul's brother, David, who was eighteen years old, delivered another route.

Paul's mother, Nora, kept the records and paid the bills. When Paul came home from school, the whole family—except for Elzira, who was only four—washed bottles. Paul learned how to look for cracks and chips on the lips of bottles.

Their farmer neighbors brought milk to the dairy in early evening, for bottling and delivery the next day.

At four o'clock in the morning, the grown-ups filled bottles for delivery. Before breakfast, sleepy Paul joined them to push paper caps into bottle tops.

Beginning in June, they chopped ice over the bottles, before Henry and David set out on their routes, so that the milk wouldn't spoil in the heat. They kept the ice in a dark icehouse, covered with sawdust so that it kept solid all summer.

By 1915, people had stopped keeping cows in their backyards. The Graves Family Dairy added customers, as trolley lines from Blue City crept closer to Busterville, bringing customers closer. People began to call Busterville a suburb.

David tried to persuade their father, Henry, to take on even more customers, hire more workers, and buy more horses.

But Henry didn't want to talk about it. "Start hiring people you don't even know," he said, "you hire trouble. Let's keep it the Graves *Family* Dairy."

"Next thing I know," Henry said to David, "you'll want me to buy one of those pasteurizing machines!"

Some city dairies had machines that heated the milk enough to kill germs before they bottled it. People could catch a disease called undulant fever from raw milk. But "heat ruins the taste of real milk," said Henry. "Besides, pasteurization is just a fad."

In February of 1916, Farmer Battle sold his land for houses and stopped selling milk to the Graves Family Dairy. Newcomers who settled on Farmer Battle's land wanted home delivery of milk.

The Graveses bought a Model-T, which David learned to drive, so that he could travel north to find new farmers. Then they hired a teamster with a Mack truck to bring them the milk.

Their milk routes were full. Paul listened as David argued that they should hire more help, add a route or two. Henry set his mouth in a line.

Another dairy started up and took on the new customers that Henry Graves had refused.

March brought a blizzard with four feet of snow. For three days, the Graves Family Dairy couldn't deliver milk by wagon. One neighbor snowshoed to the dairy to get milk for a baby. Henry asked David, "Do you think the Adlers might need milk for Peggy?" They thought of seven other customers with babies.

Paul joined Henry and David to saddle Polly and Dolly and Fred and deliver milk on horseback to families with babies.

When they returned to warm up at the woodstove, David said, "That's the best thing about being a milkman. You're bringing people something they *need*."

Henry nodded. "If we got much bigger," he said, "we wouldn't know which customers needed milk the most."

In August, the new dairy advertised in the *Blue Courier Journal* that it would pasteurize its milk beginning in the new year. A week later, an editorial congratulated this small suburban dairy for being *modern*.

Henry didn't say anything. Neither did David when he saw his father's face. Paul was surprised when his mother, Nora, spoke up, "Someday we're going to have to do it."

Early in December, David drove the Model-T, with Paul and Elzira as passengers, to visit their farmers and scout for new ones. While David and Paul inspected the Evans farm, Elzira spent the whole time petting a baby goat.

Paul was learning how to pick out the best farmers. He noticed that the Evans farm wasn't as well cared for as others. David agreed. "You'll be a good dairyman," he said.

Not long before Christmas, a great truck rolled past their house bringing the pasteurizing machine to the rival dairy.

Seven customers switched away from Graves. "They're new people from Blue," said Henry. "Probably they *like* that taste."

Winter was ice-skating time, and time for hauling ice from the pond for their icehouse. One day Elzira stayed home because her legs ached. That night she had a fever.

Then it went away.

Then it came back again, and went, and came again—in waves. With the fever she couldn't eat, she couldn't walk, and her eyes turned dull.

"What's wrong with Elzira?" Henry and Nora asked Dr. Gump.

Dr. Gump sent some of Elzira's blood to a new laboratory in Blue for testing, but it would take two weeks to get the results.

While the family waited to hear about the test, Elzira's fever shot up to one hundred and five. She talked in her sleep, babbling about the Fourth of July even though it was Christmas.

"There's a new medicine called aspirin that could help her," said Dr. Gump, "but the aspirin comes from Germany and I haven't been able to get any since the war started. Do you have any willow trees?"

"Back of the stable," said Henry, "there's Willow Creek."

The doctor told them what to do. David and Paul peeled pieces of bark from the bigger trees, and Nora boiled up some willow tea. This homemade medicine brought Elzira's temperature down.

Dr. Gump wasn't surprised. "A long time ago," he said, "the Indians knew about willow tea."

Finally, the laboratory sent Dr. Gump its report.

"What *is* it?" said Henry and Nora together.

"I thought so," said Dr. Gump, "but I wanted to be sure. You notice how her fever comes in waves? Another word for *waves* is *undulation*."

"Undulant fever!" said Nora. Henry looked miserable.

"Despite what people say," Dr. Gump went on, "it doesn't always come from cow's milk. If your milk carried the germs, your customers would get sick too. Do you keep a pig or a goat?"

The whole family said "no" at the same time.

"Well," said Dr. Gump, "she's getting better, but I wish . . ."

Paul spoke up, remembering the baby goat that Elzira had played with at the Evans farm.

Dr. Gump decided *that's* how Elzira got infected.

After the doctor left, Henry cleared his throat and announced,

"Well, I know it wasn't our milk, but . . ."

Nora said, "Bring on the pasteurizing machine."

Paul and David both smiled.

Henry looked downcast. "I guess we'll get used to the taste," he said.

Within a month, Elzira was learning to skate on Willow Creek, and

Paul let her feed Polly an apple.

For Paul, pasteurized milk was fine—as long as he could still spend mornings with Polly. In June when school was out, and he was fourteen, Paul started life as a milkman by delivering milk on a new route for cottages by the shore.

On his first morning, Paul loaded at six o'clock as the sun was rising and set out for the seaside. When he reached the first door, a customer came out to greet him in her bathrobe.

"I'm glad it's the Graves Family Dairy out here," the woman told him. "I'll never forget what you did in the blizzard."

The second day, Paul loaded his carrier and delivered eight quarts, walking from backyard to backyard in a row of cottages.

When he came out to the street from the fourth house, ready to walk back to his wagon, Paul was surprised. Polly had pulled the wagon forward and was waiting for him, looking proud of herself.

Polly got two extra lumps of sugar.

AUTHOR'S NOTE

My great-grandfather Charlie Hall fought in the Civil War and spent most of his life as a farmhand. At a mature age, working for Farmer Webb, he milked the boss's cattle and delivered raw milk to cowless neighbors. When he quarreled with his employer, he quit and took the customers with him.

Thus runs my family's creation story about the Hall Dairy in Whitneyville, part of Hamden, Connecticut. While my grandfather Henry was growing up in the 1890s, Hamden was still a country town. Then the city of New Haven's trolleys pushed out, and so did its population; people commuted from Hamden to jobs in New Haven. Under Henry's direction, the Hall Dairy grew and expanded. My father, born in 1903, was a milkman's boy, if not exactly *the* Milkman's Boy. He began to deliver milk when he was fourteen, during vacations, and later, carted it from the day his college classes stopped until the day they started up again in the fall. I was born in 1928, and by 1944 I too helped to deliver milk—lifting and carrying for a milkman who had undergone an operation.

By this time, the Halls had combined with another dairy, and I helped on a route of the Brock-Hall Dairy. I worked with Daisy; always it was the horses who labored and snorted at the center of the milkman's life. Every morning Brock-Hall horses and wagons set out pulling their white cargo, thousands of gallons over hundreds of miles.

After World War II, bright Brock-Hall trucks gradually replaced Brock-Hall wagons, and horses with hooves the size of elm stumps retreated to horse retirement—communities in the countryside—to age and grow fat and lazy.

Then came the shopping centers, and the second car. People found it cheaper to buy half gallons of milk in paper containers than to take delivery of bottles at the back stoop. Home delivery of milk dried up like a forest creek in summer's drought. Brock-Hall wavered into the 1960s losing money, then combined with another dairy, lost more money, and finally failed. Trucks went the way of horses, but to junkyards and used-car dealers rather than to fat pastures. Eighty percent of the milk sold in the 1950s was home delivered; today, the figure is one percent.

But that one percent represents more home delivery than five years ago. News stories tell about the tentative comeback of milkmen depositing glass bottles at back doors. As more and more couples work full-time, home delivery has become a convenience. But no news item notes the return of the milkman's horse.